SPACE EXPLORERS

" Then she heard a faint noise. It was as if something was creeping slowly towards her across the wet ground, making quiet, sucking sounds. She remembered about the long roots of the spear plants that feed off dead bodies.

Then it started creeping and sucking again, closer and closer … Sammi couldn't scream out loud, but somehow she screamed in her head, a scream of terror and loneliness. **"**

D1328673

SPACE EXPLORERS

David Orme

Ransom

SHADES 2.0
Space Explorers
by David Orme

Published by Ransom Publishing Ltd.
Radley House, 8 St. Cross Road, Winchester, Hampshire SO23 9HX, UK
www.ransom.co.uk

ISBN   978 178127 182 7
First published in 2003
This updated edition published by Ransom Publishing 2013

CONTENTS

ONE

Speared!

The aircraft rose up in the air, then set off across the wide plain, leaving the base camp behind it. The ground below was covered with brown grass. Prickly trees grew in clumps. They swayed in the wind that blew down from the hills. A wide river looped across the plain.

Sammi and her brother Jak lived on a

huge spaceship called the *Titan*. Their mother and father were scientists. The ship explored new planets, looking for worlds for people to live on. Younger children weren't allowed on the surface of unknown planets. But Sammi and Jak were teenagers, and were allowed to come down in the shuttle-craft to help the scientists with their work.

'Thanks for taking us on the trip, Chad,' said Sammi. Chad was a pilot. He had been sent off in a jet-powered helicopter called a buzzer. His job was to find some plant samples. He had asked Jak and Sammi along.

That's OK,' said Chad. 'But don't tell your parents. You know you're not supposed to leave the camp.'

The base camp was set up near the river. The first team to arrive had set up buildings for the scientists to work in, and a landing field for the shuttle-craft. This planet had some strange life on it, including the deadly spear plants. One scientist had been killed by them already. They looked harmless, but when someone came near they fired sharp spears at them. Then the plants sent out long suckers to feed on the dead body.

Chad pointed out a place where spear plants grew. The plants had fat, brown trunks about a metre high, then thick, swollen leaves. Some of them had red flowers. Sammi knew they were just plants, but she felt there was something evil about them. It was almost as if they could think.

'I'll go a bit lower, but not too low,' Chad said. 'I don't want to take any chances.'

'Hey, look at that!' cried Jak. The plants under the buzzer had fired off their spears. They shot upwards, then curved over and hit the ground. Luckily the aircraft was out of range.

'The noise of the buzzer must have set them off,' said Chad.

The buzzer reached the edge of the plain, where a steep cliff rose up. A waterfall tumbled down the cliff face. Soon they were crossing a land of hills.

The hill-tops were rough and rocky, but there were many deep valleys, green with plant-life. Huge, red birds soared over the jagged rocks.

Jak let out a shout.

'What's that over there?'

A grey creature was lazing in the sunshine. It was difficult to see it against the rocks.

Chad flew lower. It looked like a shaggy dog with three horns on its head. When it heard the buzzer, it stood up on two legs and headed down into the valley. It was about two metres tall.

Suddenly, there was a bang. The aircraft lurched sideways. Chad pulled hard on the controls. The buzz of the engine began to break up. The aircraft just cleared the rocks at the top of the valley. The next valley was wider. Chad spotted a flat piece of ground.

'Hang on, we're going down.'

He set down the buzzer as carefully as he could, but one side of the flat ground was soft and boggy. The aircraft tipped over. The engine stopped with a final splutter.

Chad jumped out of the buzzer and looked underneath it.

'What happened?'

A long, green pole was sticking into the base of the machine.

'We must have passed over a spear plant in that valley. This spear's gone right through the power cell. I am so stupid!'

Sammi climbed out.

'How will we get back?'

'Not in this machine. I'll have to radio back to the base.'

He groaned. 'I'm going to be in so much trouble over this! I'll be up in front of the captain in the morning!'

Jak climbed out of the buzzer. 'Are there any spear plants round here?' he asked.

'Yes, there's one over there. It fired at us when we came down. There's no need to worry though. Once they've fired their spears, it takes them a few days to grow new ones.'

Chad climbed back into the buzzer. 'Buzzer nine to base. Chad Mason here. We have problems. Come in please.'

Nothing but a hiss came from the machine. Chad tried again.

Again, there was no reply. Sammi felt a horrible feeling inside. Would they have to walk back? What about the spear plants out on the plain?

'Is the radio broken?'

'No. It's this deep valley. The radio signals are being blocked. Now I want you to wait here and keep the doors shut. I'm going to take the radio to the top of the hill.'

Chad jumped out of the buzzer and started to climb.

Two hours went by.

Chad hadn't come back, and the day was coming to its end.

TWO

Night Strangers

'What are we going to do now?' said Jak.

Sammi didn't know. She couldn't imagine what had happened to Chad.

'Chad must be in trouble. We ought to go and look for him.'

Sammi agreed.

'We'll climb up the hill to see what has happened.'

Sammi opened the door and stepped out into the squelchy mud. Jak jumped down beside her. Nearby, the spear plant loomed. Luckily it had used up its spears. Its big flower buds waved gently, even though there was no wind.

One of the buds was almost open. Yellow pollen drifted from it.

Suddenly, they smelt a strange perfume. Then everything seemed to go woozy. The yellow pollen had reached Sammi first. She fell to the ground. Soon Jak was stretched out on the muddy grass as well.

Sammi and Jak couldn't move. They felt sick and dizzy, but they were still awake. Hours passed, and the valley grew very dark. Jak tried to pretend it was all just a horrible nightmare.

Sammi thought about the spear plant. Would they still be lying there when the plant grew new spears?

She seemed to sleep for a while, and then woke again. She was very cold. The sky was lighter now. The light came from the planet's two moons.

Then she heard a faint noise. It was as if something was creeping slowly towards her across the wet ground, making quiet, sucking sounds. She remembered about the long roots of the spear plants that feed off dead bodies.

What if this was a sucking root, creeping towards her across the mud? Maybe, when the plants had fired all their spears, they used the strange pollen instead to catch their prey. Only their victims were not dead, just paralysed, waiting for the roots to get nearer and nearer …

For a moment the creeping sound stopped, and Sammi told herself that it couldn't be a root. Nothing could grow that quickly, surely? But then it started creeping and sucking again, closer and closer …

Sammi couldn't scream out loud, but somehow she screamed in her head, a scream of terror and loneliness. Then she must have blacked out again, because the next thing she knew was the feeling of being lifted up. She felt herself being put on a stretcher of some sort. A smelly cloth, like a rough blanket, was draped over her face. She tried to speak, but her lips and tongue still would not move.

She was carried for a long time. Then she felt the stretcher being carefully put down. She fell again into a deep sleep.

When she woke there seemed to be more light. Above her, she could see a roof made of jagged, grey rock.

To one side there was a bright patch of

light. The mouth of a cave. But what was she doing in a cave?

She looked again at the bright area of light, and, as she did so, a figure stepped into it.

It was tall, taller than anyone she had ever seen. And on its head there were three horns.

THREE

Alone

The creature was coming closer, blocking out more light.

Sammi sat up. Jak was fast asleep next to her.

'Jak! Wake up! It's one of those horned things!'

Jak scrambled to his feet and started walking towards the horned being. He did not seem to be frightened.

This was too much for Sammi. She screamed.

The creature knelt down on the floor, looking like an animal in pain. Could Sammi's scream have hurt it? It had shown the signs of pain just before she had screamed. The creature turned and scrambled out of the cave.

'Why did you do that?' said Jak. 'She was only trying to help us.'

'How do you know? How do you know it's a *she* anyway?'

'I just know.'

'You can't know. They could kill us, eat us … *anything*.'

'Of course they won't. Come on, let's go and tell her it's all right.'

Outside the cave, they saw that they were in a shallow valley. Below them was a village.

Small, stone houses were scattered around a central square. The buildings were simple but they were solid and well-made, with wooden shutters for windows.

A larger building of two storeys stood next to the square. A wide stream ran through the village. Many of the horned people were filling big pots with water from it. A group of children were splashing about.

Jak thought of them as people rather than creatures. Sammi wasn't sure. Fear flooded her mind again. As if they could feel her fear, the whole village stopped what they were doing and turned to look at them.

'Come on.' Jak was off. Sammi wanted to call him back, but he seemed so sure of himself. She shrugged her shoulders and followed him.

The horned people seemed happy to see them. Some of the young ones had come running up.

Brother and sister were led to the square in the centre of the village. Here there were rough seats made of planks. They sat down and were surrounded by horned people of all ages.

'How do you know which ones are male and which ones are female?' Sammi asked Jak again.

'I just do.' He pointed to two of the children.

'They're both boys, but that one over there is a girl.'

Sammi was too polite to stare closely at them, but there really didn't seem to be any difference. She wondered again how Jak was so sure, but he couldn't explain any more than he had.

In the middle of the square was a large fire. Two adults were fixing a skinned animal onto a long pole. The animal was to be cooked for supper. Sammi felt sick. You didn't get fresh meat on space ships. It upset her to see an animal being roasted.

Sammi really wanted to find out how Jak seemed to know so much about these people. He found it hard to explain.

'I just feel it in my head,' he said.

'You mean you can read their minds?'

'No, of course I can't!'

It was difficult for Jak to explain to his sister what was happening to him. For some reason it was something that he could do, but she couldn't.

'I just knew they were friendly. And some of them feel female and some male. I can't explain it. And they can feel what we are feeling. Like when you were upset in the cave. You were frightened and your feelings really hurt her.'

Sammi still didn't understand.

'Do you mean they can read our minds? That's horrible.'

'No, I don't. I don't think they can, anyway. They just feel things.'

Jak wouldn't say any more. Sammi was still not sure about the horned people, and didn't like the idea of them knowing what was going on in her head, even if it was just feelings. She also didn't like the idea of Jak being able to do something she couldn't. It made her feel left out.

It was well after dark before the food was ready. Someone started cutting up the meat with a sharp knife made from a flinty stone.

The two humans were given a plateful of meat and vegetables on a rough, wooden plate. They were surprised at how good it was.

Sammi looked up. A bright dot was crossing the sky. It was the *Titan* in orbit. She felt even more lonely. She began to cry quietly. Instantly, the alien people all knew she was unhappy. They started to stroke her face and arms.

Then something happened. The worst thing she could imagine. A great roar echoed from over the hills, and two new stars, red and flickering, rose up.

'The shuttles! They're going back! Oh Jak, why are they leaving us here?'

FOUR

The Store-house

The horned people picked up Sammi's terror. They all looked upset. Sammi and Jak were marched back to their cave, where their feelings of fear were blocked out by the rock.

Jak was furious.

'Why did you do that? You've upset them!'

'But the shuttles. Don't you see? They're going off without us!'

'Dad would never let them do that.'

Sammi thought so too, and yet there had been no rescue party, no buzzers flying over, nothing at all.

Sammi felt she couldn't sleep, but worry had made her tired. It was difficult to get comfortable, but soon they were sleeping. Outside, the horned people had settled down again. One of them was playing a sad tune on a stringed instrument.

Suddenly, the sky was lit up by a flickering red light. It hung in the air, then died away. The whole village jumped up, pointing and speaking in their quiet voices. They had no idea what this strange light could be. Sammi and Jak would have known that it was a distress flare, but they were sleeping.

Sammi and Jak came out of their cave

cautiously the next morning. They expected the villagers to be angry with them, or even march them back to the cave. But the events of the previous night seemed to have been forgotten. Everyone was friendly, as brother and sister made their way down the path.

They were hungry, and the horned people seemed to know. There was some greasy, cold meat left over from the night before, and Sammi and Jak were given this, along with what looked like lumpy porridge. Even Sammi ate all she was offered.

They set off for a walk round the village. Jak seemed perfectly happy, and Sammi couldn't understand why. Didn't he realise that they could be trapped here on the planet forever?

'Look, Jak we can't just stay here. We've got to do something.'

'Like what?'

'We could try to speak to them. Maybe they could help us look for Chad.'

'But we don't know their language.'

'I know that. But you seem to know what they're thinking. That's a start.'

'I keep telling you, I *don't* know what they're thinking. Sometimes I know what they feel.'

The female who had come to them in the cave when they had first woken had been especially friendly. From the way the other people acted, it seemed that she was an important person. Even Sammi could recognise her, for she had a red streak of fur on one arm. As they walked back to the square, they met her. Sammi thought that she would try speaking to her.

She pointed to one of the houses and said 'house'. Red-arm caught on almost at once.

She pointed to the house and mumbled something. Sammi tried to say it back to her. Red-arm made no attempt to say 'house'.

Sammi tried again. She pointed to the fire-pit, and said 'fire'. She got a different mumble in return. This seemed an easier word, and Red-arm looked pleased when Sammi tried it. Sammi then pointed to her chest, and said, 'Sammi'. Red-arm pointed to her chest and made another whispering, mumbling noise. Sammi tried it.

Red-arm was interested now, although she didn't try to repeat any of Sammi's words. She pointed to her head, her arm, her horns, and her legs. Each time she made a different noise. Finally, she tapped her chest and made the first sound again. Sammi groaned.

'It's not her name. It must be the word for

"chest" she's saying. We're not getting anywhere!'

Red-arm saw that the game was over for now and she patted Sammi on the arm, then disappeared into one of the houses.

Horned people came to their doors as Sammi and Jak walked past. Everyone was busy. Outside one house, clay pots were drying in the sun on wooden racks. Inside another, a loom could be heard clacking away, making brightly-coloured blankets.

They headed for the tall building by the square. The doors were open. People were sitting outside in the sunshine, some on benches, some on the ground. They were busy with a number of tasks: preparing food, mending blankets, making tools out of wood and stone.

Sammi wondered whether they would be

allowed inside the building. She peeped in. No one seemed to mind, so they went in.

The building was the village store-room. The ground floor was stacked high with objects: a heap of spears, hides from various animals, stacks of tall jars containing seeds.

Although there were small windows all round, it was gloomy and they very nearly missed the familiar object lying in the middle of the floor.

It was the radio Chad had taken with him when he left them three days before.

FIVE

The Radio

'Chad's radio! How did that get here?'

'If only we knew how to work it,' said Sammi.

'No problem,' boasted Jak. 'I've seen them being used dozens of times.'

They took the radio outside. Jak pressed *transmit*.

'Anyone there? Come in please.'

There was no reply.

'We might be on the wrong frequency,' he said. There was a panel of buttons, but despite his boast, Jak had no idea what any of them did. He pressed one marked *out-station call*. A few moments later they heard a voice.

'Hello, who's there? This is Chad Mason, and I'm lost. Come in please!' Jak pressed the transmit button again. 'Chad, this is Jak. I'm here with Sammi. Where are you? Over.'

'Jak! Are you two OK? You must have found the radio. I slipped on some rocks and banged my head not long after I left you. I dropped the radio and couldn't find it. I blacked out after that. When I woke up I was sitting on a mountainside and there was no sign of the radio. I've been wandering around lost for two days. Where are you?'

Sammi took over and tried to tell him their story. Of course, they couldn't tell him where they were, for they had no idea.

'How can you talk to us Chad, if we've got the radio?'

'I've got a pocket out-station unit. You must have pressed the call button, and it beeped at me! These units don't have a big range, so you can't be far away. Look for a switch called *homing*. Set that to *on*. My unit has got a direction-finder, so I can find my way to you.'

Sammi found the button and pressed it. A few moments later Chad spoke again.

'I'm on my way!'

Sammi spoke again. 'Chad, didn't you see the shuttles taking off last night?'

There was a pause. 'Yes, I saw them. I'm not sure what's going on. Don't worry, I'll be with you as soon as I can.'

Jak and Sammi decided to leave the radio in the store-house. If they took it with them to the cave, the homing signal might be blocked.

Sammi spent the rest of the afternoon trying to talk to the horned people, but without much luck.

Jak had been thinking. 'I think I know why you couldn't get Red-arm to say her name.'

'Why?'

'None of them have names. They don't need them, because they know each other by the way they think and feel.'

'Why can't *I* tell what they're feeling?'

'I don't know. I can only do it a bit. I'm not very good at it. Maybe you need horns to do it really well.'

Evening had come and the great fire had been lit, when the children heard the sound of scrabbling on the rocky path. The villagers jumped up in alarm and stood with their horns pointing in the direction of the sound. Chad walked into the firelight, and immediately the alarm was over. The musician carried on playing. The villagers knew that Chad meant no harm, and that he was tired, hungry and thirsty.

He waved to Sammi and Jak.

'Hi guys! Is there a spare dinner for me?'

One of the horned people brought a plate of food. Chad thanked them very politely and, although the villager didn't understand Chad's words, the message was clear enough.

Chad was interested in how the horned people knew what they were feeling.

'We've come across people like this on other planets. They're called empaths. They can't read minds, but they can tell when someone is hungry, or frightened, or in pain. It means they can find each other when they are in trouble. Jak can do it a little, even if he doesn't have the horns. Pity that, a couple of horns would suit him.'

'Why do you think they didn't rescue you as well as us?'

'They probably found you when I was knocked out. My brain wasn't sending out messages, you see. The ones that found you must have found the radio. Anyway, where is it?'

They went to the store-house and Chad checked the radio over.

'Everything's working OK. I should be able to get a signal to the *Titan*, but I'll have to wait until it's overhead.'

Chad set the radio up on a rock. He looked at his watch.

'We should see the *Titan* crossing over in

about five minutes.'

They waited five minutes, ten, twenty, but no bright star passed over the valley.

The *Titan* was no longer in orbit round the planet.

SIX

On the March

The fire was flickering low. The musician played a last, sad tune. Sammi had a coldness in her stomach, which nothing could shift. Not wanting to upset the village people, she had gone back to the cave, her sadness blocked by the rocky walls. After a while, Chad and Jak joined her. Chad tried to be cheerful, but it was difficult when he couldn't understand why they had been left on the planet.

Suddenly, there came a repeat of last night's flare, burning red in the dark sky. Chad jumped up excitedly.

'Hey guys, it's a flare. Someone still loves us out there!'

Sammi and Jak crowded in the entrance, watching the flare dying away. They cheered and clapped their hands. Most of the villagers had gone back to their houses. The villagers still sitting round the fire danced and waved too. Even the musician took out his instrument again and played a cheerful tune. Chad checked the direction with his compass.

Now we know what direction to move off in in the morning. Go and get some sleep now – you're going to need it.'

The next morning they were ready to set off. A path climbed out of the valley going in roughly the right direction.

The villagers seemed worried. They kept getting in the way. Soon they were surrounded by the horned people and couldn't move.

'What's going on?' growled Chad. 'Come on, out of the way.'

But the horned people wouldn't move. They simply stood there, muttering quietly.

After a while, Chad and the children turned and walked back into the valley. The horned people fell back.

'They don't want us to go,' said Jak. They're protecting us. It's dangerous outside the valley. They don't want us to get hurt.'

'Well, we can't stay here forever. We'll rush them this time. Just stroll around, then when I say go, rush for the path.'

When 'go' came they ran as fast as they could, but the villagers were quicker, and a group of grey, furry bodies were soon blocking the way.

Sammi became upset.

'Why won't you let us go?' she yelled, beating at one of the villagers with her fists. 'Don't you understand? I WANT TO GO HOME.'

The horned people began to move away, some of them clutching their horns. The three humans moved forward. This time, no one tried to stop them. When they reached a point half-way up the hill, Jak stopped and turned. He raised his hand and waved. The horned people held up their arms, knowing somehow that it was his way of saying goodbye.

They set off across a stony plain, broken

up by deep valleys full of plant-life. These were dangerous and they avoided them. Although it was sunny, a cold wind was blowing. There were no paths to follow, but Chad kept them roughly on track with his compass.

After walking and scrambling for over three hours, they stopped for a rest. They had reached a pile of rocks and could shelter from the wind. Chad handed out a ration of water and some high-energy food tablets.

'No sleeping,' said Chad firmly. 'I don't know how much further we have to go and I don't fancy too many more nights out in this cold. Come on, let's move.'

Jak put his hand down to push himself up. Immediately, he cried out in pain.

'Something has bitten me!'

Chad grabbed at Jak's hand, looking

worried. Bites on unexplored planets could be serious. An angry, red mark showed up on Jak's thumb. A scuttling noise came from between the rocks and a small creature disappeared into the shadows.

Chad broke out the medical kit and slapped a dressing on the thumb.

'How does it feel?'

'It stings a bit.'

They set off again. After half an hour Chad stopped and checked Jak. He didn't like what he saw. Jak's hand was puffy, and red marks were spreading up his arm.

'How do you feel now?'

'OK, I think.'

After another ten minutes it was clear that Jak was in trouble. His arm was throbbing, and he felt dizzy.

I need to sit down for a minute,' he said.

'OK. Take a break, you two. I'm just

going as far as that high point up ahead.'

Jak lay down with his back against a smooth rock. He just wanted to curl up, somewhere out of the cold wind, and sleep …

Chad went on to the high point to get a view of the way forward. When he reached the top, he almost cheered. They had reached the edge of the hills. He could see the ground falling away to the wide plain, with the broad river sweeping across it. In the distance, on the site of the scientist's camp, something stood out on the plain. It was one of the *Titan*'s shuttles! There were no people or buildings. But if they could reach the shuttle …

He looked at the route they would have to take with his binoculars.

Everywhere he looked across the wide plain, clumps of spear plants stood like armies of menacing soldiers.

SEVEN

Down River

Chad guessed that the pollen from the spear plants had affected the base, just as it had affected Sammi and Jak. He remembered how the flowers of the plants had been opening as they flew over them. It must be the beginning of the flowering season. The wind off the hills would have blown the pollen right across the base.

When there was nothing but silence from the base radio, a rescue party would have come down to see what was up. If everyone at the base had been unconscious, they wouldn't be able to report where the missing buzzer had gone. The shuttle had been left behind, just in case they were able to reach it. The nightly flare was automatic, set up to guide them back.

Jak was dozing now, shivering slightly.

'He's pretty bad, isn't he?' said Sammi.

Chad nodded.

'Yes, he's bad. But we're nearly at the plain, and there's a shuttle left for us at the base. But there's a problem.'

He handed Sammi the binoculars. He wanted her out of the way for a while, so that he could have a good look at Jak's arm.

The whole arm was swollen now. The red

marks ran in streaks up to the elbow.

Jak opened his eyes.

'Is it hurting, Jak?'

Jak didn't speak. He just nodded, then closed his eyes again.

Chad heard footsteps. He thought Sammi had returned, but it wasn't Sammi. It was Red-arm. Behind her stood two more horned people. They had followed them all the way from the village. In all his years exploring strange planets, Chad had never met such caring people. If only humans could be more like them!

Red-arm kneeled down and traced the red marks down Jak's arm to the tiny wound in the thumb. She looked at Chad, then flattened the palm of her furry hand and drew it across Jak's shoulder. The meaning was clear. If Jak were to be saved, the arm would have to be cut off.

Just then, Sammi returned. For once, she was pleased to see the horned people, especially Red-arm. Sammi trusted her.

'Is Jak very bad? What was she trying to tell you?'

'She thinks the arm will have to come off if he is to be saved. They're probably right.'

Sammi's eyes widened with shock. 'But how? There's no hospital here, and nothing for the pain. If only we could get Jak back to the *Titan*!'

She set off back to the high point, waving at Red-arm, making her follow. When they got to the top she pointed towards the distant shuttle, and with all her heart she longed to be back at home on the ship. The grey woman gazed across the plain, and slowly she understood.

Red-arm led them down the cliff. A stretcher had been made for Jak from a blanket and two spears, and the two other horned people carried him between them.

When they reached the bottom of the cliff, Red-arm turned sharply to the right, following a new path. Ahead of them they heard water splashing.

They squeezed between two boulders and saw a waterfall tumbling down the cliff face into a pool. A wide stream flowed out of the pool and there, tucked between the rocks, were three canoe-like boats. Chad and Sammi got into one. Jak was gently laid into another. One of the horned people travelled with Chad and Sammi, Red-arm was in Jak's boat, while the third horned native travelled in the last boat. Each boat had a paddle covered with animal fur.

Soon they were off, drifting gently downstream. There was a strong current, so the paddle was used only for steering.

The river widened as other streams ran into it. The rocks gave way to sandy banks.

Chad noticed that no spear plants grew near the river. He wondered if the soil was too damp for them. He was still worried about the yellow pollen, for this could travel a long way in the wind. He guessed that the pollen was triggered by noise, like the spears.

It was a silent place, apart from the wind off the hills, which never seemed to let up. It was as if every creature that lived there crept around on tiptoe to avoid upsetting the spear plants. The boats were designed to be completely silent.

At last, they arrived at the nearest point to the base. It was about five hundred metres from the river. No spear plants grew near the river bank, but there was still a hundred metres of plants for them to cross.

The horned man who had travelled alone stepped out of his boat. He was carrying something that looked like a drum. He put a blanket over his head, then started to crawl silently towards the spear plants.

Slowly, slowly, he crept towards the bristling plants. Chad guessed that the blanket was soaked in something to protect him from the pollen. But what about the spears? The slightest noise would mean death.

On and on he crept. At last, he reached the spear plants. He tucked himself underneath the big, fleshy leaves. Carefully, he reached out from under the blanket and began banging loudly on his drum.

EIGHT

The Shuttle

The horned man pushed Chad and Sammi
down into the boat and threw a stinking
blanket over them. Red-arm covered up Jak.
They could hear the swish of spears and the
thud of them hitting the ground. Then
came more drumming, followed by more
swishings and thuds, further away this time.

Sammi felt sick under the smelly blanket,

but she managed not to be. Another minute passed, and the horned man climbed out of the boat. He tugged on their arms. They stepped out onto the bank, keeping the blanket over their heads.

Sammi found that she could just see her way by looking through the cloth. The air was full of pollen, but the blanket protected them. The drummer came to meet them, still wearing his blanket.

Soon they were walking through the spear plants. They had fired off all their spears at the sound of the drumming, so it was safe. Chad was helping Red-arm with Jak's stretcher. When they reached the gate, the horned men stopped.

It is difficult to say goodbye to people who have helped you so much, especially when you can't speak to them. Sammi held Red-arm's furry hands and realised that she didn't need to speak. Sammi felt she knew what she was thinking, although it was feelings rather than words. And the feelings said, 'Good luck. Come back to us soon.'

Chad and Sammi carried Jak to the shuttle. When they reached it they turned back, but the horned people had gone.

The door swished open. They squeezed into the tiny airlock, closed the outside door, and waited while the air was changed. On this planet, with its dangerous pollen, this was vital.

At last, they were able to throw off the blankets. Chad sat down at the radio.

'It may take quite a while to raise anyone,' he warned. 'It depends how far away *Titan* is.'

He flicked over the switches.

'Chad Mason to *Titan*. Come in please, *Titan*.'

To his surprise a voice came back almost immediately.

'*Titan* here. Who is with you? Over.'

'I'm with Sammi and Jak Ward. Jak is sick and needs immediate attention. Where are you? Over.'

'We're round the back of one of the moons.'

Chad wasted no time before taking off. The sky above grew darker and darker. Chad nudged Sammi and pointed. A star was growing brighter as they watched. The *Titan*!

As soon as they were in the shuttle dock, medical staff rushed in to collect Jak. All three of them were taken straight to the ship's hospital.

The hospital was very crowded. Beds full of sleeping people were squeezed in all over the place. In the middle of it all, Mum was waiting for them.

Sammi rushed to her, and they both wept. Mum looked anxiously down at Jak before he was rushed away.

'I thought I had lost all my family,' Sammi's mother said.

'What do you mean, all your family? What about Dad?'

Sammi's mother led her to one of the beds. Dad lay there sleeping, surrounded by flashing machines.

'All of the people from the base are like this. We know it was the pollen from those plants, but the doctors haven't been able to wake them up.'

'But we know how to. Quickly, get those smelly blankets out of the shuttle airlock!'

A few minutes later a crewman appeared, carrying the rough blankets.

'We were just about to burn these,' he said.

Doctors clustered round. The filthy, smelly blankets looked out of place in the spotless hospital. Sammi explained how the horned people used them.

Dr Ward was the first patient for the treatment. The blanket was laid over him. For some hours nothing happened.

The captain came to see them. He explained why the *Titan* had moved behind the moon.

'You should have remembered the most important rule of exploring space,' he said. 'Intelligent races of people must be left alone and not disturbed. Contact with a more advanced race can be very dangerous – we've learnt that from Earth history. When we first arrived, we didn't know about the horned people. One of the other pilots found them just after you did, so we had to move fast – it's amazing what the sight of an extra star in the sky can do sometimes.'

'But what about the flares?'

The captain looked uncomfortable.

'I wish you hadn't mentioned that. Your mum was very persuasive. It doesn't actually mention flares in the rules, but whatever you do, don't tell anyone!'

Jak woke first. His arm had almost returned to normal, and his doctor was looking very pleased.

'It was a pretty wild poison,' he said. 'Soon matched it up, though. Another hour, and things could have been tricky.'

Then they heard a cheer coming from the bed where Dr Ward lay. He was also coming round.

He was weak and groggy, but getting better. 'What happened?' he asked.

Sammi laughed. She didn't know where to start.

Blitz

by David Orme

During World War Two Martin is evacuated to Winchester. He hates it there, and manages to find his way back home to London. But home isn't where it used to be – a bomb has exploded in his street, destroying his house. What future is there for Martin, homeless in a bombed-out city?

Fire!

by David Orme

It is 2nd September 1666 in London and Martin Outwich is suddenly awoken by the sounds of fire. He thinks nothing of it, but the fire is spreading and very quickly the whole city is ablaze. Abandoned by his master, Martin must race across the city to save himself and his sister Martha. Will he make it in time?

Gateway from Hell

by David Orme

To Lisa and her friends, Mott Hill is sacred, so they are determined to stop a new road being built on it. But something ancient and dangerous, maybe even deadly, lies below Mott Hill. And it has been disturbed.

Plague

by David Orme

It is 1665 and the plague has hit the city of London. Life will never be the same again for apprentice apothecary Henry Harper. His father is dead and his mother and brother have fled the country. Can Henry escape from the city he loves before the plague strikes him?

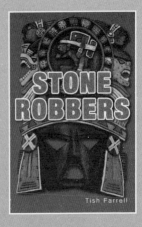

Stone Robbers

by Tish Farrell

Rico's dad is dead, after a long fight to preserve his Mayan heritage. Now Rico hates everything to do with it. His family have been left extremely poor and his sister Delfina has to sell produce in the city to earn money. Then swindler Enzo tries to cheat the family out of their hard-earned cash. Will Rico manage to get revenge?

Life of the Party

by Gillian Philip

Chloe spends her spare time binge drinking with her friends, much to the disgust of Rob, a boy from school who fancies her. One particular drunken night, after an argument with her best friend Steph, Chloe manages to stagger home, but the next morning awakes to something much worse than a hangover.